THE MONSTER
MAC AND CHEESE
PARTY

TODD PARR

Megan Tingley Books

LITTLE, BROWN AND COMPANY
NEW YORK BOSTON

This book is for all the monsters that lived under my
bed when I was little. I'm glad you weren't real.

About This Book

The illustrations for this book were created on a drawing tablet using an iMac, starting with bold black lines and dropping in color with Adobe Photoshop. This book was edited by Megan Tingley and designed by Jessica Dacher. The production was supervised by Virginia Lawther, and the production editor was Marisa Finkelstein. The text was set in Mikado and hand-lettering from the author, and the display type is Mikado.

YOU ARE INVITED
TO
A MONSTER
MAC and CHEESE PARTY
FRIDAY NIGHT!
PLEASE BRING YOUR

FAVORITE MAC and CHEESE.

WARNING!

NO
HUMANS
ALLOWED!!
MONSTERS DO NOT
LIKE MACARONI
AND CHEESE MADE BY
HUMANS! (IT'S BORING.)
NO HUMANS!   OR ELSE!

(ONLY MONSTERS ARE ALLOWED
TO EAT THE FOOD IN THIS BOOK!)

It's almost time for the party to start.
The monsters are very hungry!

Where is everyone?

The bat is here. He brought his favorite
macaroni and cheese. Bat mac 'n' bugs!

Here comes the witch.
What did she bring?

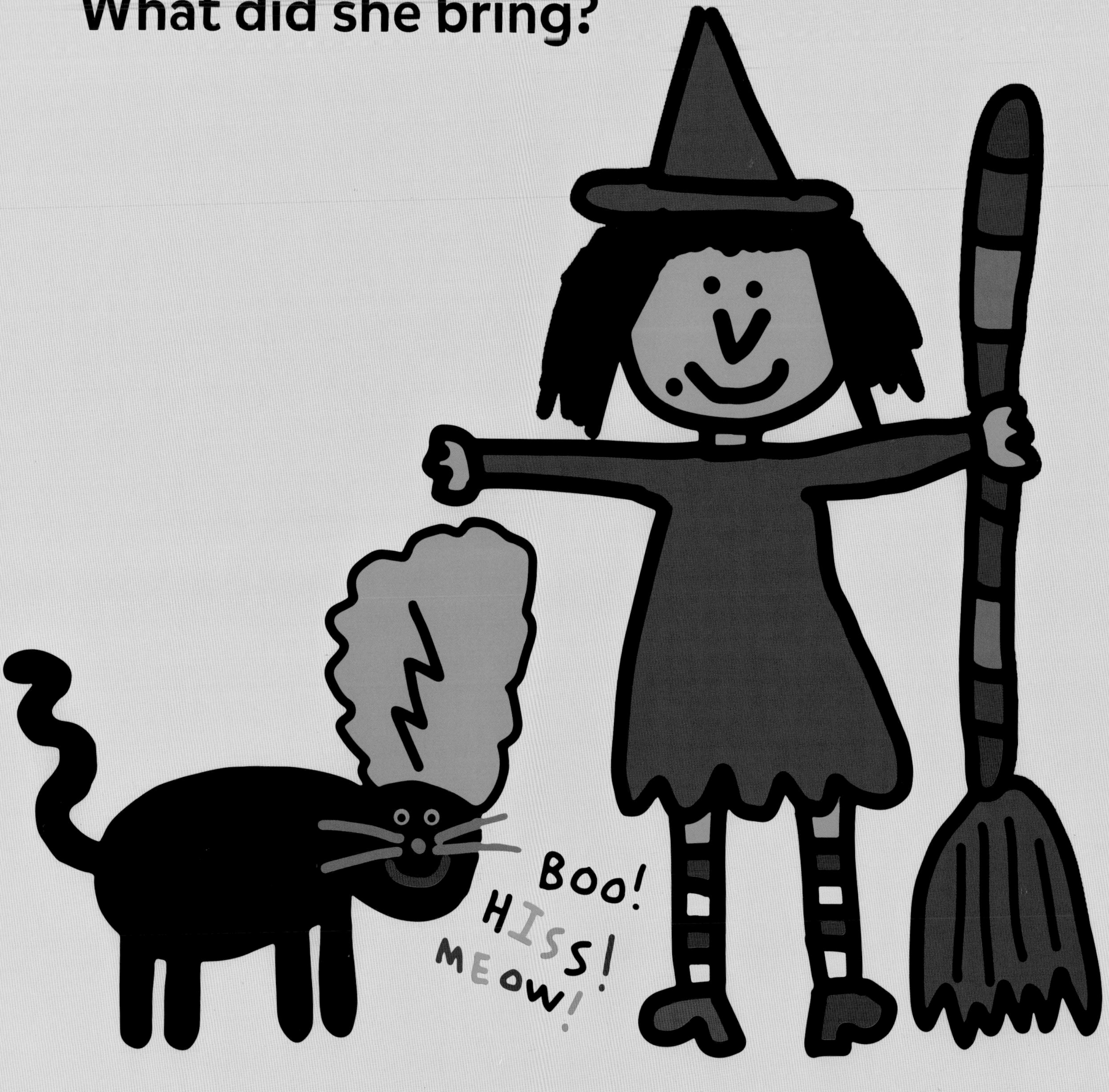

**Glow-in-the-dark mac with
snakes and furballs.**

The sea monster is here with
her mac and cheese.

In the bathtub, of course!

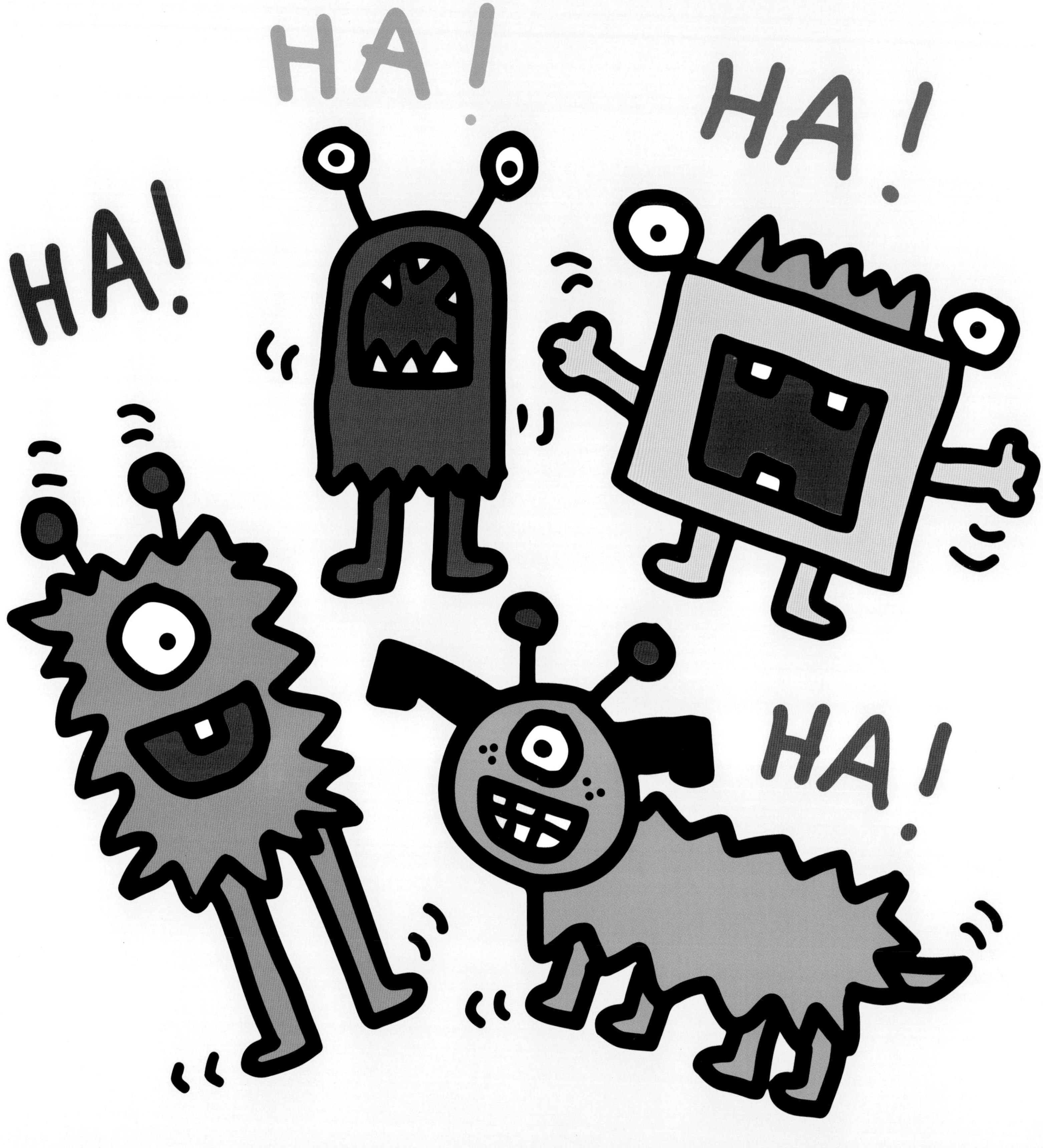
HA!
HA!
HA!
HA!

The zombie has arrived!

He brought zombie mud mac with fingers.

Here are the werewolves.

They brought howling macaroni
and cheese with bones.

MAC AND CHEESE WITH STINKY SOCKS?
MAC AND CHEESE MADE WITH PLANTS AND BEANS?
MAC AND CHEESE WITH UNICORNS?
MAC AND CHEESE WITH HOT DOGS?

The spider is here. What did she bring?

Spider mac with flies.

The mummy has arrived with . . .

...mummy mac with eyeballs!
Would you eat that?

**DING.
DONG!**

Who could that be?
All the monsters
are already here.

It's the HUMANS! They brought their favorite mac and cheese. FROM THE BOX!

What's wrong with HUMANS?

NOTHING!
WE JUST LIKE TO
MAKE OUR OWN
MACARONI AND CHEESE!
(BUT WE LOVE HUMANS!) LET'S EAT!

HA! HA! HA!

Sharing a meal can be lots of fun. It's good to try new things 🍰 and make new friends. 👾👾👾

THE END. LOVE,

Todd ♡

I ♥ mac and cheese so much that I wanted to share my favorite recipes for you to make with an adult human. Have fun and save me some leftovers

TODD MAC

8 OZ PASTA
¼ CUP BUTTER
1 CAN (12 OZ) EVAPORATED MILK
CHEESES (½ CUP EACH, SHREDDED):
    CHEDDAR
    AMERICAN
    SWISS AND/OR GRUYÈRE

Cook pasta as directed. Drain. Add butter and milk. Stir in all the cheeses. Add salt and pepper to taste. Eat!

VEGAN MAC
GLUTEN-FREE

8 OZ GLUTEN-FREE PASTA
1 TSP VEGAN BUTTER
½ CUP NUTRITIONAL YEAST
¼ TSP SMOKED PAPRIKA
¼ TSP GARLIC POWDER
¼ TSP TURMERIC
½ CUP VEGAN CHEESE
½ CUP CASHEW CREAM

Cook pasta as directed. Drain, but save some pasta water on the side. Add butter, yeast, paprika, garlic powder, and turmeric. Stir in cheese and cashew cream. Use some of the leftover pasta water if it's too thick. Add salt and pepper to taste. Eat!

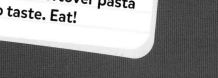